Cinderella

Disney

Hachette

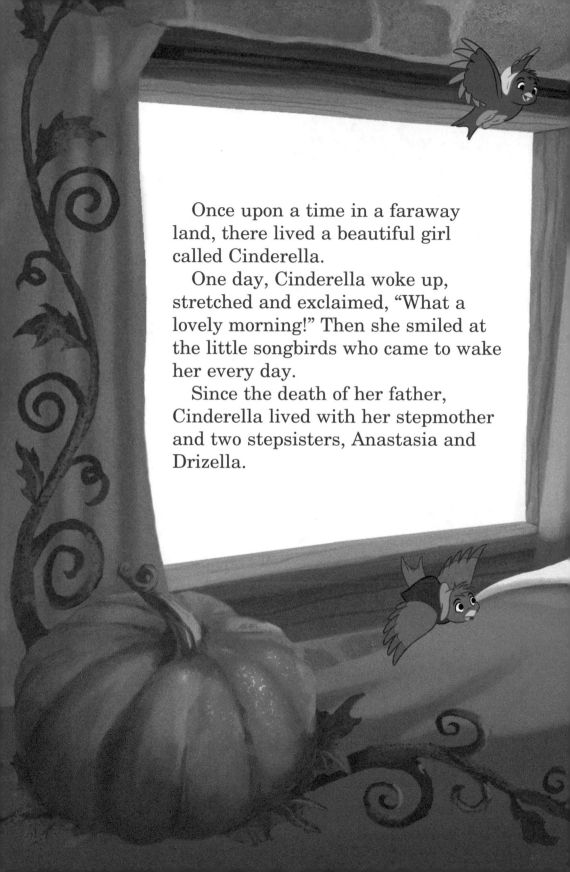

Once upon a time in a faraway land, there lived a beautiful girl called Cinderella.

One day, Cinderella woke up, stretched and exclaimed, "What a lovely morning!" Then she smiled at the little songbirds who came to wake her every day.

Since the death of her father, Cinderella lived with her stepmother and two stepsisters, Anastasia and Drizella.

Poor Cinderella was treated
worse than a servant in her
own home. Her stepmother
made the girl spend all
day long cooking, sewing,
scrubbing and dusting,
while Cinderella's two
lazy stepsisters never
lifted a finger to help.

One day, a royal messenger came to the house with a letter from the King. There was to be a ball that night, in honour of His Royal Highness the Prince. Every eligible maiden in the land was commanded to attend.

"We're going to meet the Prince!" yelled Drizella.

Cinderella smiled. She had always dreamt of attending a grand ball.

"That means I can go too!" exclaimed Cinderella. Anastasia and Drizella burst out laughing. "Can't you just picture her, dancing with the Prince?" said Anastasia spitefully. She mocked Cinderella with glee. "Would Your Highness be so good as to hold my broom?"

"I see no reason why you can't go," said the Stepmother slyly. "*If* you can finish all your work and *if* you can find something suitable to wear."

Once she had finished her chores, Cinderella rushed to her room. She rummaged through an old trunk and pulled out a ballgown that had belonged to her mother. "Isn't it lovely?" she said to her friends, the mice Jaq and Gus.

"Maybe it's a little old-fashioned, but I'll soon fix that," said Cinderella. She took out a book of dress designs. "There ought to be some good ideas in here," she said as she turned the pages. "I can shorten the sleeves, add a sash, a ruffle and a collar, and then I'll have..."

Then came a familiar cry from downstairs: "CINDERELLA!" Cinderella sighed. She would have to wait before she could begin working on her gown.

"Why haven't you finished your work?"
demanded the Stepmother.
"But I have," protested Cinderella.
"No, you still have to polish the floors and clean
the windows," ordered the Stepmother. "I want
them gleaming!"

Cinderella got to work, but she was interrupted by her stepsisters' never-ending demands.

"Mend the buttonholes!" demanded Anastasia, dumping a pile of clothes in Cinderella's arms.

"Press my skirt too. And mind the ruffle, you're always tearing it!" added Drizella.

"Work, work, work," said Jaq. "She'll never get her dress done."

"Poor Cinderelly," agreed Gus, shaking his head.

The mice and the birds got together and decided that they would all help their friend.

"We'll make a lovely dress for Cinderella!" they all agreed.

Gus and Jaq sneaked up to the stepsisters' bedroom as they were getting ready for the ball.

"This sash! I wouldn't be seen dead in it!" moaned Anastasia.

"And these beads – I'm sick of looking at them," shouted Drizella, as the two of them flung all their things on the floor.

Gus and Jaq saw their chance to sneak away with the beads and the sash. But half-way through the mission, Lucifer the cat woke up and saw what they were up to. The two little mice had to use all their cunning and bravery to outwit him.

At last they made it safely back to the attic with their treasures.

Swiftly and skilfully, many nimble beaks and tiny paws went to work on Cinderella's gown. Soon, they had transformed the old dress into a magnificent ballgown.

By the time Cinderella had finally finished her chores, it was time to leave for the ball.

"Why, Cinderella, you're not ready," said the Stepmother.

"I'm not going," sighed Cinderella.

"What a shame," sneered the Stepmother. "But of course, there will be other balls..."

Cinderella sadly climbed the stairs to her room.

"Oh well," she said to herself. "What's all the fuss about a royal ball anyway? I suppose it would be dull and boring and... completely wonderful."

Then Cinderella opened the bedroom door and couldn't believe her eyes.

"Surprise!" the birds and mice shouted together.

Cinderella thought her gown was the most beautiful she'd ever seen.

"Thank you, thank you so much!" she exclaimed to her friends.

In an instant, Cinderella put on her gown and raced downstairs to join her stepsisters.

Anastasia and Drizella couldn't believe their eyes! Then the Stepmother looked more closely at Cinderella's outfit. "These beads... they add just the right touch. Don't you think so, Drizella?" she asked sneakily.

Drizella peered at the necklace. "Why, you little thief!" she shrieked.

"And that's my sash!" yelled Anastasia.

Drizella yanked the necklace from Cinderella's neck, while Anastasia ripped the sash off, tearing the gown to rags.

Then the three women swept out of the room. Cinderella stood, too shocked to move, in her ruined gown.

Cinderella ran crying into the garden. She was sure that her dreams would never come true now.

Her animal friends had never seen Cinderella look so sad.

"There's nothing left to believe in," sobbed Cinderella.

"Oh, you don't really mean that," a soft voice replied. "If you'd lost all your faith, I wouldn't be here. And here I am!"

Cinderella looked up and there, in front of her, was an old woman. It was her fairy godmother!

"Dry those tears," she told Cinderella. "You can't go to the ball looking like that."

"The ball?" said Cinderella, astonished.

Everything the Fairy Godmother needed to help Cinderella was already in the garden – a pumpkin, a horse, a dog and the mice.

"Bibbidi-bobbidi-boo!" commanded the Fairy Godmother, and in an instant the four mice were transformed into handsome white horses.

Another "Bibbidi-bobbidi-boo!" and the pumpkin turned into a beautiful coach. "Bibbidi-bobbidi-boo!" The horse became a smart coachman. And with a final "Bibbidi-bobbidi-boo!" the dog was transformed into a footman!

Now it was Cinderella's turn. With a wave of her magic wand, the Fairy Godmother changed Cinderella's rags into a beautiful ballgown. Cinderella loved her dress. "And look – glass slippers. Why, it's like a wonderful dream come true!"

But the Fairy Godmother had a warning: "Don't forget that on the stroke of midnight the spell will be broken and everything will be as it was before!"

As Cinderella's magic carriage raced towards the royal palace, the King was in despair. He had organised the grand ball so that his son, the Prince, could find a bride.

But the Prince didn't seem to be interested in
any of the girls that he was introduced to.
Just then, Cinderella made her entrance.

The instant he caught sight of her, the Prince was in love. She was the girl of his dreams! He asked the mysterious girl to dance with him.

Cinderella accepted the Prince's offer and the couple danced gracefully around the ballroom to the tune of a beautiful waltz.

Everyone watched in amazement.

"Do we know her?" asked Drizella.

"The Prince certainly seems to!" replied
Anastasia.

"There's something familiar about her," said the
Stepmother thoughtfully.

The Prince and Cinderella spent the rest of the evening dancing and talking.

Suddenly, Cinderella caught sight of the watchtower clock.

"It's nearly midnight!" she gasped. "I must go. Goodbye!"

Cinderella ran off down the steps as fast as she could.

"No, wait!" the Prince called after her. "Please come back!"

But Cinderella kept running. She was in such a hurry to leave before everything changed back that she lost one of her glass slippers.

The Prince showed the glass slipper to the Grand Duke.

"Find the girl who wore this slipper!" he ordered. "She's the girl I want to marry!"

Meanwhile, at the final stroke of midnight, Cinderella and all her friends had changed back to normal. All she had left to remind her of her wonderful evening was one of the glass slippers.

The next day, there was
a royal proclamation. The
Prince was searching the
kingdom for the girl who
owned the glass slipper,
so that he could make her
his bride.

When she heard the news,
Cinderella gasped with joy. Her
handsome dancing partner was
the Prince! Unfortunately, the
Stepmother guessed the truth.

The Stepmother followed Cinderella and locked her in her room, putting the key in her pocket.

"Let me out!" protested Cinderella.

"We've got to get that key!" cried Gus and Jaq.

Using all their cunning, they managed to sneak the key from the Stepmother's pocket.

Painstakingly, the two mice hauled the key to the top of the stairs. They had to fight off Lucifer but finally, they managed to slip the key under Cinderella's door.

Meanwhile, the Grand Duke had arrived at the house. Drizella and Anastasia were both determined to claim the glass slipper and marry the Prince!

Drizella tried on the slipper first. "There! It's exactly my size!" she declared. But the slipper was much too small.

Then it was Anastasia's turn, but her foot was too big, just like her sister's.

"You are the only ladies in the household, I presume?" said the Grand Duke. "There's no one else, Your Grace," lied the Stepmother.

Just as the Grand Duke turned to leave,
Cinderella appeared at the top of the stairs.

"May I try it on?" she asked. The Grand Duke
agreed, but as the footman brought the slipper to
her, the Stepmother tripped him up with her stick.
The slipper smashed into tiny pieces on the floor!

"Oh no!" cried the Grand Duke.

Then, to the Grand Duke's astonishment,
Cinderella brought out the other slipper. And it
fitted her perfectly!

So Cinderella and her handsome Prince were married, and everyone in the whole kingdom rejoiced in their happiness, especially Gus and Jaq.

At last, Cinderella's dreams had come true!

Cinderella

The Stepmother

Drizella

Anastasia

Jaq and Gus